CHUCKY THE LONELY INUKSHUK

STORY BY JUDITH MCMURRAY

ILLUSTRATED BY D. A. DUNFORD

WITH

THE TOBIN ISLAND SCHOOL OF FINE ART
LORETTA ROGERS
DARCEY SILLS
KAREN GENOVESE
SUSAN GOSEVITZ
SIMON DUNFORD, JUNIOR MEMBER
MEGAN TORISAWA, JUNIOR MEMBER

THIS BOOK IS DEDICATED TO MY GRANDSON

RYAN PIERCE TORISAWA

WHOSE JOY OF LIVING

ALWAYS INSPIRES ME

Front Cover: *"Inukshuk"*, by D.A. Dunford
Back Cover: *"Red Canoe"*, by Simon Dunford
Edited and designed by Cynthia McMurray
Photography by Scott Turnbull, Turnbull Photography
Printed in Canada at Friesens

First printing 2009
ISBN 978-0-9813819-0-9

Published in 2009 by Bryler Publications
Box 1035,
Chester, NS
B0J 1J0
902-273-2286

All Proceeds From This Book Will Be Donated To The Juvenile Diabetes Research Foundation

dedicated to finding a cure

The International Diabetes Federation estimates over 246-million people worldwide are diagnosed with diabetes every year. Sadly, 70,000 of these are children with juvenile (type 1) diabetes, a condition that strikes suddenly and without warning. In Canada alone, close to 300,000 Canadians live with type 1 diabetes, marking Canada with the 6th highest incidence rate of type 1 diabetes in children 14 years or younger in the world.[1] In fact, we now know type 1 diabetes is rising by as much as five percent each year, the greatest increase being in children between the ages of 5-9.[2]

Diabetes has been around since the days of the early Egyptians. Ancient physicians as far back as the 3rd Dynasty make reference to the disease. Today however, researchers estimate by 2025, globally, over 380-million people will be diagnosed with diabetes.[3] Currently, statistics show almost 4-million people worldwide die each year from the disease.[4] And if a cure is not found soon, this number is only expected to rise.

While all forms of diabetes can cause devastating complications, type 1 diabetes is especially concerning because it affects so many children, making them dependent on daily insulin shots simply to survive. This destructive disease attacks the pancreas, leaving it unable to produce little if any insulin, a necessary hormone responsible for many important metabolic functions within the body. Although we simply don't know the exact cause of type 1 diabetes yet, scientists believe it causes the body's own immune system to attack and destroy the vital insulin-producing cells within the pancreas. Unfortunately, for children living with type 1 diabetes, this means enduring daily insulin injections, which can amount to almost 1,460 needles a year and another 2,190 finger pokes to test their blood sugar levels. Simon Dunford is one of these children.

Simon, now 14, was first diagnosed with type 1 diabetes when he was only five-years-old. Like many children with this disease, Simon takes daily insulin injections and must constantly monitor his food intake. Simon is like most 14-year-old boys in every other way, except soon, he will also wear an insulin pump that will automatically inject the vital insulin into his body. Despite the disease, Simon has learned to cope with life as a child living with diabetes. He is already an amazing artist and has contributed two beautiful paintings to this book.

Chucky the Lonely Inukshuk is in part dedicated to finding a cure for type 1 diabetes, and to all children like Simon who must endure the complications and devastating effects of this disease. The author, artists and many others involved in the making of this book, have generously donated their time, work and all proceeds from the sales of the book to the Juvenile Diabetes Research Foundation of Canada (JDRF). JDRF is the leading charitable funder and advocate of type 1 diabetes research worldwide. The association was founded in 1970 by the parents of children with juvenile diabetes. Since then, JDRF has provided more than $680 million in direct funding to diabetes research worldwide.

For more information or to make a charitable donation, visit the JDRF web site at www.jdrf.ca or call 1.877.CURE.533.

1. UN WHO Gold Report 2006
2. As above
3. International Diabetes Federation, Prevalence and Projections
4. International Diabetes Federation, 2007 Mortality Rates

Chucky the Inukshuk stood alone on a large gray rock in the middle of a deep lake in Northern Ontario.

Chucky stood silently, as he had done for years, watching as the small waves slowly crept up his stone toes and back out again toward the dark blue water.

"Inukshuk"
by D.A. Dunford

Chucky was actually made a very long time ago by Inuit travellers.

He helped them navigate the huge lake.

Today, Chucky is an extremely proud Inukshuk.

He always stands TALL, looking out over the water with a serious stare.

He is made of many different size stones that form his arms and legs.

The Inuit people picked a very special stone for Chucky's head

to make sure all the travellers would recognize him.

You see, Chucky has the most important job on the lake.

His tall, strong body tells boaters exactly where they are.

Everyone who crosses the WIDE lake knows Chucky stands

straight off the point of a heavily treed island

so they can always find their way home.

"Pink Muskoka" by Loretta Rogers

"Paddling Out" by Simon Dunford

Chucky knew he symbolized safety, hope
and friendship to everyone who saw him.

But what travellers didn't realize is that Chucky was also very lonely.
He had been standing in the same spot for many years,
guarding the lake and its travellers.

Boaters passed him by almost every day
but no one ever waved or stopped to say hello.

To this day, the Inuit people believe Chucky is a silent witness to those who pass before him
and a BEACON to those who have yet to come.

One day, as Chucky stood looking out over the beautiful blue lake,
he heard the rumble of distant thunder.

A thick fog slowly crept in, covering the trees.
Lightning suddenly lit up the sky with a brilliant white light
and Chucky instantly knew a **THUNDERSTORM** was brewing.

Chucky actually looked forward to the storm
because the pouring rain always scrubbed his big body of rocks clean.

In between the **rumbles** of thunder,
Chucky thought he heard a child's cry.

He listened very intently and then he heard it again.

"Help, help".

"Early Mist on Rosseau" by D.A. Dunford

"Stormy Waters" by Susan Gosevitz

It wasn't long before Chucky saw a lone, shiny, red canoe bouncing in the growing waves.

The young children, who now held on very tightly to the rim of the canoe, passed by him every day on their way to sailing camp.

He immediately recognized the familiar blonde hair of the ten-year-old twins.

The young boy and girl always seemed very polite and nice children
but they never stopped or waved to Chucky as they paddled by.

They ignored poor Chucky as he stood alone
on his LARGE gray rock in the middle of the lake.

Right now however, they were paddling their canoe
as fast as they could straight toward him.

The children seemed very frightened.
They knew the storm was fast approaching.
They also knew they were in danger out alone on the lake.

They needed shelter.

"Paddling to Safety"
by Darcey Sills

Soon, the little boy and girl were at Chucky's feet.

They quickly pulled their shiny, **red** canoe out of the water and onto the rocks.

Now, the *storm* was very near.

The lightning danced in the clouds above,
casting an **eerie** glow on the dark blue lake.

With each flash of brilliant light, the autumn trees
cast red and orange shadows that seemed to skip across the water.

Chucky sensed the children were very afraid.

"Approaching Storm" by Darcey Sills

The waves grew bigger and soon they began to SPLASH up onto the rocks.

The anxious brother and sister hung tightly to Chucky's body for safety.

Chucky felt very **brave** and strong as he watched over the children, keeping them safe from the pounding waves.

Although both children remembered to wear their life jackets, they were very cold and started to **shiver**.

"Chucky Comforts the Twins"
by Loretta Rogers

Although is seemed like the storm would last forever to the frightened children, after a little while, the lightning began to subside and the growling thunder became only a murmur in the distance.

The dark clouds, too, began to pass and a beautiful blue and pink light filled the afternoon sky.

The storm had passed and the children were safe.

"Diamonds on the Water" by D.A. Dunford

The anxious ten-year-olds slowly climbed down from Chucky's body.

They searched for their shiny, red canoe but it was nowhere to be found.

The crashing waves had carried it out onto the lake.

"Now, what are we going to do?" the boy asked his still very frightened sister.

The little girl began to cry. She was very cold and hungry.
Large tears rolled down her face, falling at Chucky's feet.

As she looked down, she suddenly noticed something sticking out of the rocks.

The little girl started to move the small rocks around Chucky's very large toes.
After several minutes, she found a root that smelled just like licorice!

"Inukshuk" by D.A. Dunford

The children put the funny looking plant to their tongues and tasted it.

It tasted very good!

Looking up at the huge Inukshuk, the little girl smiled, imagining for a moment Chucky had left a great big box of her favorite licorice just for her.

"Licorice Dreams"
by Megan Torisawa

As Chucky looked down at the children, he remembered a story about a kind boater who planted the roots between the rocks on his little island many years before the Inuit travelers had created him. The caring man hoped that some day his gift would flourish, helping a stranded traveller in need of food.

"Summer on the Lake"
by Loretta Rogers

The children started to feel so much better as they chewed on the tasty root, they didn't even notice an interested **turtle** watching them as they munched happily on their newfound treat.

"Would there be any left for him?" he wondered, as he slowly crept up the rocks toward them.

"Curious Turtle" by Megan Torisawa

It wasn't long before the sun
poked through the last
of the passing clouds.

Chucky felt the sun's warm
rays on his stone face.
He sighed with relief as it
shone brightly on the calm,
blue water below.

He was very happy to see
the sun was also
warming the children's
cold little bodies.

He knew everything
would be okay.

"Lake Muskoka"
by Susan Gosevitz

"Relieved" by D.A. Dunford

As Chucky looked out over the lake, he suddenly spotted a boat heading toward them.

It was the children's very worried parents.
They had been looking for the children for hours.

As you can imagine, the parents were very relieved to see their children huddled together on a rock as the giant Inukshuk stood over them.

Chucky noticed the father was holding a long rope attached to the shiny, red canoe the waves had pulled onto the lake during the storm.

As the parents reached the little island, the very grateful twins turned to Chucky.
They both put their tiny arms around him and hugged him tightly.
They thanked him for holding onto them and keeping them safe during the frightening storm.

Chucky was very happy.

He stood proud and tall, watching the family wave goodbye as they paddled home.
Soon, a thin smile appeared on his strong stone face.

To this day, Chucky the Inukshuk continues to stand guard
from his large gray rock in the middle of a deep lake in Northern Ontario.
And if you look very closely, you can still see his tiny grin.

"Heading Home" by Karen Genovese

So, whenever you feel alone or frightened, remember Chucky, and know he is **watching** over you, too.

"Summer Dreamer" by D.A. Dunford

Colour Me

For contest rules and instructions on how to enter, visit: www.brylerpublications.com

Colour Me

For contest rules and instructions on how to enter, visit: www.brylerpublications.com